NO LONGE
SEATTLE P

DRILL TEAM
DETERMINATION

BY JAKE MADDOX

text by
Cindy L. Rodriguez

STONE ARCH BOOKS
a capstone imprint

Published by Stone Arch Books, an imprint of Capstone.
1710 Roe Crest Drive
North Mankato, Minnesota 56003
capstonepub.com

Copyright © 2022 by Capstone. All rights reserved. No part of this publication may be
reproduced in whole or in part, or stored in a retrieval system, or transmitted in any form
or by any means, electronic, mechanical, photocopying, recording, or otherwise, without
written permission of the publisher.

Library of Congress Cataloging-in-Publication Data is available on
the Library of Congress website.

ISBN: 9781663910998 (hardcover)
ISBN: 9781663920249 (paperback)
ISBN: 9781663910967 (ebook PDF)

Summary: Thirteen-year-old Aniyah comes from a long line of steppers. Her family doesn't
understand why Aniyah doesn't want to continue the tradition. But Aniyah doesn't like
performing. Then Aniyah's friend Stacy convinces her to give step club a try. Aniyah
discovers that stepping is fun! But just when Aniyah is starting to get into the groove, the
rules change, and the club decides to enter drill team competitions. Can Aniyah overcome
her fears and get on board with performing, or will she have to step away from drill team?

Image Credits:
Alamy/Tetra Images, cover and throughout; Shutterstock, design elements

Editorial Credits:
Editor: Kristen Mohn; Designer: Bobbie Nuytten; Media Researcher: Svetlana Zhurkin;
Production Specialist: Katy LaVigne

TABLE OF CONTENTS

CHAPTER I

THE FAMILY TRADITION

Aniyah Lewis answered the front door a dozen times, welcoming friends, family, and what seemed like half the neighborhood to her family's annual Labor Day party. She delivered the guests' bowls, crockpots, and endless bags of chips to the kitchen. She smiled each time an aunt, uncle, or cousin arrived, but she really wanted her best friend, Stacy, to get there.

When Aniyah saw Stacy's mom's car finally pull up in front of the house, she ran outside. "It's about time," called Aniyah.

Stacy lifted up her wrist and looked at it. She wasn't wearing a watch, but she said, "I think you mean I'm right on time."

Aniyah shook her head. Both girls waved as Stacy's mom pulled away, then they ran around the side of the house and into the backyard. Aniyah led Stacy to an open area on the grass, weaving through the adults who were laughing, eating, and talking.

"Red or blue?" Aniyah asked when they had made their way to the cornhole game.

"Red," said Stacy, picking up the red beanbags. "And I go first."

"Oh no you don't," Aniyah said. "I've got home field advantage."

The girls laughed and then settled into a rhythm. They took turns tossing beanbags high and long.

They aimed for the hole in the center of the wooden platform. One of Aniyah's tosses went wild and hit a party guest on the head as he bit into his hot dog.

"Sorry, Mr. Riggs!" Aniyah called out. The girls giggled as Mr. Riggs tossed the beanbag back to them—under his knee, basketball style.

After a while, Aniyah's mom walked over to the girls with two plastic cups filled with lemonade.

"Hi, Mrs. Lewis," said Stacy.

"Hello, Stacy." Mrs. Lewis handed each girl a cup. "So, who's winning?"

Stacy shrugged, and Aniyah said, "We're not keeping score."

"Really?" asked Mrs. Lewis. "When I was younger, my sisters and I couldn't even go to the park together without competing somehow. We'd be walking, and then one of us would start running. Suddenly, we'd be in a race to see who'd get there first."

"You're *still* like that," said Aniyah. "I heard all of you arguing about whose potato salad was the best!"

Mrs. Lewis laughed. "We weren't arguing," she said. "It was a friendly debate. And FYI, mine's the best." She winked at Stacy.

Aniyah heard loud laughter behind her. She turned and heard her aunts chant, "Hold up, wait a minute." This was followed by a series of stomps and claps.

"Oh, no," sighed Aniyah.

"Oh, yes," said her mom. She speed walked across the yard to join her three sisters. "You can't start stepping without me!" she yelled.

"What's going on?" asked Stacy.

"Come on," Aniyah said reluctantly. "You'll want a front row seat when they stomp down memory lane."

Stacy stared, wide-eyed, as the women lined up next to each other. Aniyah's mom counted, "Five, six, seven, eight," and then, in sync, she and her sisters stomped their feet onto the concrete patio. They smacked their hands on their thighs between each step.

"Wow!" said Stacy as she watched.

Aniyah leaned over and whispered to Stacy, "They all went to historically Black colleges and competed on drill teams."

Aniyah's dad took a break from his grilling duties to cheer and clap along.

"Does your dad step too? Looks like he wants to join in!" said Stacy.

Aniyah laughed. "No. He didn't go to a historically Black college," she said. Like Stacy, Aniyah's dad was white. "And he doesn't know how to step."

"Yup. We've still got it," said Aniyah's mom as the women fell easily into a routine they had mastered a couple decades ago.

"Yes, you do!" shouted Aniyah's dad, who went back to flipping burgers on the grill.

"Where are the boys?" asked Aunt Gabby.

Without hesitation, Uncle Maurice cupped his hands around his mouth and shouted, "Alpha Phi Alpha is in the house!" He stomped his way over to the women. After a few steps, though, he grabbed his hip dramatically, as if in pain.

"You better go easy, old man," warned Aunt Kayla.

Everybody laughed. Uncle Maurice did a quick two-stomp to prove he was fine and still had moves.

"That was awesome!" shouted Stacy when the performance ended.

Aniyah shook her head hard and said with a laugh, "No. No. Please don't encourage them."

Aunt Gabby fanned herself and took a sip of her drink. "Whew. It's not as easy as it used to be.

It would be nice to see the next generation step up and carry on the family tradition."

Aniyah's mom gave her daughter a look. They had talked about this very thing before.

"It's a sore subject, Gabby," Aniyah's mom said. "Aniyah isn't interested."

"It's not that I'm not interested," Aniyah said with a sigh. "I just hate to perform or compete in front of people. My anxiety takes over, and I panic."

Stacy's eyes went superwide, and she whacked Aniyah on the shoulder. "Our school has a step club that doesn't compete," she said. "It's just for fun. We should join this year!"

Aniyah shook her head and gave Stacy a hard look that meant *Stop talking*, but it was too late. Aniyah's aunts surrounded the girls and swallowed them in a group hug.

Aniyah's mom shouted, "That's perfect! I'm so excited you're going to learn how to step!"

When did I agree to this? wondered Aniyah, but she didn't say anything.

When the group hug ended, Aniyah and Stacy walked back to the cornhole game. Aniyah stared at Stacy while she tossed her beanbag in the air and caught it over and over.

"What?" asked Stacy. "It could be fun!"

"You don't understand," Aniyah insisted. "Stepping is my mom's thing. Not mine."

"It could become *our* thing," said Stacy. "Come on. We're going to be in eighth grade. We should try something new."

Aniyah rolled her eyes.

"It looks like fun. I want to try it, and I don't want to go alone," Stacy said. "Promise you'll come with me to the first meeting. It's your job to support your best friend. . . ." She gave Aniyah a cheesy smile, folded her hands in a begging motion, and blinked rapidly for effect.

"Fine," said Aniyah. "I'll go with you to the first meeting, but I'm not making any promises beyond that." She tossed her bean bag and sunk it in the hole. "Three points," she said.

CHAPTER 2

WELCOME TO STEP CLUB

On the Monday of the first full week of school, Aniyah kept her promise and met Stacy outside the gym at three o'clock for the step club's first meeting.

"You're here!" said Stacy as she gave Aniyah a bear hug.

"Of course, I'm here," Aniyah replied. "I promised you, right?"

"Ready to go in?" asked Stacy.

"Not really," said Aniyah. But she took a deep breath, wiped the palms of her hands on the sides of her shorts, and entered the gym behind Stacy.

Ms. Soto, the eighth-grade history teacher, stood just inside the door. "Welcome, girls," she said. She handed the girls a clipboard and a pen so they could sign in.

"Thanks!" said Stacy.

Aniyah smiled weakly.

"Is this your first time stepping?" Ms. Soto asked.

"It is for me, but Aniyah comes from a drill team family," said Stacy.

Aniyah froze in place. Her stomach flipped, and she gripped the straps of her backpack so hard that her knuckles turned white.

Great, thought Aniyah. *Now, Ms. Soto is going to think I know more than I do. I just want to stand in the back and not be noticed.*

When Ms. Soto looked at her expectantly, Aniyah swallowed hard and forced a smile.

"That's great," Ms. Soto said. "But don't worry, Stacy. We have all levels. Lots of girls here today are new and have no experience. We'll start with the basics and build from there. Plus, these aren't tryouts. We're a no-cut group."

"Whew!" Stacy said with a laugh. "So, what should we do?"

"Go over and join the others," Ms. Soto said. "We'll start in a minute."

Aniyah and Stacy walked to the center of the gym, joining the large group of chatting, laughing girls. Aniyah recognized many of them. Soon, Ms. Soto walked over and stepped up onto the first row of the bleachers to get their attention.

"Welcome to step club, everyone!" she said. "Before we begin, I want you to appreciate what you're doing. Step has a long history in the Black community. Its roots trace back to the African gumboot dance. Black fraternities and sororities have been stepping on college campuses since the early nineteen hundreds."

Ms. Soto paused a moment and held her arms out to the group in front of her. "Today, all races and ages step and add their own twists, including props, tumbling, and music. The core of it is simple, though. Your body is the instrument. You make music with your stomps, claps, and smacks. And the people around you are your bandmates. The Swahili word for unity is *Umoja*. When you step, you are unified by your moves and your purpose."

Aniyah noticed the girls in the front row were nodding.

"Plus, it's a whole lot of fun," Ms. Soto said with a big smile. "Are you ready?"

The front-row girls snapped to attention and said, "Yes, ma'am!" They were clearly the ones who knew what they were doing.

"I asked, are you ready?" repeated Ms. Soto, louder.

The rest of the girls straightened their spines and shouted, "Yes, ma'am!"

"That's better!" yelled Ms. Soto. She hopped down off the bleachers and said, "Count off one to five so we can create five smaller groups."

Aniyah walked over to her group, bummed that she and Stacy weren't together. One of the front-row girls, a fellow eighth grader named Jasmine Torres, appeared to be in charge.

Aniyah didn't know Jasmine well, but they had been in some classes together over the years. She knew Jasmine was Afro-Dominican and spoke fluent Spanish. She was taller than Aniyah, and her dark hair was tightly braided on one side and left natural on the other. Aniyah's hair was similar, but her curls were looser since her dad's hair was pin-straight.

Jasmine had the girls form a semicircle in front of her so that each girl could see her easily. She led them through their first series of stomps and claps.

"I always talk out the moves when I'm trying to learn them," said Jasmine. "It might sound silly, but it works for me. Like this . . . stomp, clap, stomp, clap, stomp-stomp, clap-clap."

Everyone watched her. It seemed easy because she did each move super slowly. But Aniyah knew from watching her mom and aunts that the steps would speed up eventually.

"Try it with me," said Jasmine. "Start with the right foot. Ready? Right foot stomp, clap. Left foot stomp, clap. Then right-left, stomp-stomp, clap-clap. Easy, right?"

Everyone watched as Jasmine added to the routine and picked up the pace. "Stomp, clap, stomp, clap, stomp-stomp, clap-clap," she said.

Then Jasmine's body exploded into a series of new moves. She lifted each leg four times, clapping under her lifted knee each time. She stomped and clapped in front of her body and then stomped and clapped behind her back. She hunched over a bit and turned her arms, lifting one straight into the air, while the other was bent and held close to her body. Then she switched it up and dabbed down and then up and down on the other side, all while pounding one foot or the other onto the gym floor.

When Jasmine stopped, she looked at the semicircle of stunned faces. She smiled and said again, "Easy, right?"

The girls, including Aniyah, laughed nervously. Aniyah wasn't surprised by Jasmine's moves because she had seen them her whole life. But she had always just watched. Now, the thought of doing the steps herself, as perfectly as her mom, made her anxious.

Aniyah glanced over and caught Stacy's eye. Aniyah shook her head and gave her friend a look that said, *How did I let you talk me into this?*

Stacy returned a look that said, *It's gonna be great!*

Jasmine slowed things down and walked the girls through the moves, one step and clap at a time. She said each move out loud as she did it. "Knee up, clap, stomp. Other knee up, clap, stomp. And really step—hard! We're not tiptoeing through the tulips here. We're stomping!"

At the end of the hour, Aniyah was breathing hard. The soles of her feet felt like they'd been pummeled.

Ms. Soto asked the girls to line up again in front of her. Before she stepped up onto the first row of the bleachers, she huddled with the small group of girls who were leading the drills.

"Great job today, everyone! Give yourselves a hand," Ms. Soto said.

Aniyah was all clapped out by then, but she managed a polite golf clap to join the others.

"Before you go, I have a big announcement to make," said Ms. Soto excitedly. "We have been a noncompetitive club since we began three years ago. My veterans and I agree, though, that it's time to take the club to the next level. We now have the numbers, and based on what I saw today, we have the talent.

This year, the Northwest Middle School Step Club will become a competitive drill team!"

While the girls around her erupted in cheers and high fives, Aniyah stood motionless.

"What do you say, Northwest Drill Team?" shouted Ms. Soto. "Can we do it?"

"Yes, ma'am!" the girls shouted. Aniyah remained quiet.

"I asked, can we do it?" repeated Ms. Soto.

"Yes, ma'am!" the girls thundered louder.

"Great! We will practice every Monday and Thursday after school. Our first competition is in six weeks, and we will have one every month after that." said Ms. Soto.

As soon as Ms. Soto dismissed them, Aniyah headed for the door. Stacy ran after her.

"Aniyah, wait up!" Catching up with Aniyah, Stacy asked, "Hey, what's wrong?"

"You know how I feel about performing in front of crowds and competing against other teams," Aniyah said. "I can't breathe. I get dizzy. I feel like I'm going to be sick. I can't do it. I agreed to come to the first meeting to make you and my mom happy. I kept my promise, but now I'm done."

"Come on, Aniyah. We'll learn the routines, we'll practice, and in six weeks, we'll be ready."

"*You* will be ready," said Aniyah. "I'll be cheering for you from the stands."

Stacy opened her mouth to say more, but Aniyah stopped her. "I'm serious, Stacy. I'm sorry, but I really can't."

Stacy looked down and said, "Fine."

The girls were quiet as they walked outside and waited for the late bus. They remained quiet the whole ride home.

CHAPTER 3

FINISH WHAT YOU START

As Aniyah sat down for dinner, her mom asked, "How was step club today?"

"Um, it was fine," said Aniyah.

"Is that all we're going to get?" asked her dad. "Come on. Give us some details."

"Yeah," said her mom. "How many girls were there? Did you learn any routines? Show us your new moves!"

"Nope. Not gonna happen," said Aniyah. "Please pass the corn."

"You're no fun," her mom said as she handed Aniyah the bowl of buttered corn. "At least tell us about it."

Aniyah reluctantly reported the details to her parents, telling them about the twenty girls who'd been there. She also described the basic moves they had practiced.

"Sounds like a great start," said her mom.

"Yeah, it was fine," said Aniyah. "But I'm not going back."

"What?" asked her dad, setting down the forkful of pork chop he'd been about to eat.

"Why wouldn't you go back?" added her mom.

"Step club is suddenly drill *team*—and they're going to compete," explained Aniyah. She mashed kernels of corn under her fork and watched the juice ooze out.

"And?" her mom prodded.

"And you know how I feel about performing or competing in front of people. I get so nervous that I feel sick."

"Oh, honey, I know. I sympathize. I really do," said her mom. "I remember when you were supposed to be in the *Three Little Pigs* play in third grade. That morning, you woke up in tears. I know your fear is real."

"Exactly," said Aniyah. She let out the breath she had been holding.

"But . . . ," her mom continued.

Oh, no, thought Aniyah. *So much for having sympathy and understanding.* She braced herself for what her mom would say next.

"There will be times in your life when you will have to perform in front of people," Mom said.

Aniyah looked to her dad for some help. Once in a while, that worked. Aniyah would widen her big brown eyes in a way that said, *Save me*, and her dad would jump in to defend her.

This time, though, he nodded and said, "Mom is right, Aniyah."

Aniyah put her fork down, crossed her arms, and slouched in her chair.

"You'll always have oral presentations to do in school, and you'll have job interviews when you get older," said her mom. "That's just for starters."

"'All the world's a stage, and all the men and women, merely players,'" Dad added, quoting Shakespeare.

Aniyah sighed and slumped down even farther.

"We are always performing, really," said her mom. "And you can't avoid competition forever. Sometimes it's healthy. You have to learn how to manage your fear and push through it. Knowing how to stick with something, even when it's difficult, is a skill worth learning, Aniyah."

"Okay, but I don't have to learn that *right now*. Maybe next year when I start high school," Aniyah suggested with a small, hopeful smile.

"Actually, you have to do it now. You promised Stacy you would join the team with her," Mom reminded her. "You know one of our family rules is to finish what you start."

"Hold on. I promised her I would go to the first meeting, which I *did*," said Aniyah. "I didn't make any promises after that. Actually, I already told her I couldn't go back."

"And how did that go over?" asked her dad.

"She was fine with it," said Aniyah, avoiding eye contact.

Her mom gave Aniyah a hard stare.

"Okay, she *said* it was fine . . . but she's probably disappointed," Aniyah admitted.

"Uh-huh. Is that the kind of friend you want to be?" asked her mom.

Aniyah looked to her dad again. His eyes were sympathetic, but he just gave a small shrug. Aniyah didn't even bother to argue about it anymore. She knew it would be a waste of breath.

"Let's compromise," said her mom. "Keep going to the practices with Stacy. When it's time for the first competition, we'll see how you feel. Wait until then to decide. Deal?"

"Fine," said Aniyah. "I'll text Stacy tonight and tell her." She picked up her fork again and pushed the food around her plate. She wanted to get up and go to her room, but she had to finish what she started. She shoved a forkful of corn into her mouth, even though her appetite was gone.

CHAPTER 4

WHAT'S IMPORTANT NOW

On Thursday after school, Aniyah dragged herself into the gym at the start of practice. Stacy ran up to Aniyah and jumped on her back.

"I know this isn't going to be easy for you," said Stacy. "Thank you so much for coming back. I really don't want to do this without you."

Aniyah smiled as Stacy hopped down from her piggyback ride. "Well, since I *have* to do this, I'm glad I'll have my best friend here for support."

Stacy smiled back and gave Aniyah a goofy double thumbs-up.

Ms. Soto called for everyone's attention. "Today, we are going to practice the same steps you learned last time," she said. "Instead of being in small groups, though, we are going to step as a team. The goal is for all of us to be synchronized. Remember the word *Umoja*—unity. It's not easy for a group this big to move as one. I don't expect it to happen right away. It will take lots of practice."

She paused and looked over the group of girls. "Let's line up in four rows of five."

The girls moved into position. Aniyah had placed herself in the back row.

"Are we ready?" Ms. Soto asked.

"Yes, ma'am!" the team shouted.

Ms. Soto cupped her ear, a signal that meant she wanted them to be louder.

"Yes, ma'am!" they yelled with more volume.

"First row, remain standing. Everyone else, have a seat. Our veterans will perform the first part of the routine twice. The first time, they will go through each move slowly. They'll call out the step's name, like they did last time. The second time, they will do it quickly, so you can see what it looks like when everyone is in sync."

Jasmine, the eighth grader who'd led Aniyah's group the first time, stood in the middle of the first row. She raised her arms in front of her, chest-high, and thrust her balled her fists together.

"Ready?" she called.

Each of the girls in Jasmine's row also lifted their arms out front and held one fist against the other. This was their "ready" stance.

Then Jasmine said, "Ready, and . . ."

A second later, the girls all started the routine. They went slowly, naming each move as they did it. Stomps, claps, dabs, squats, smacks, and poses. They also named the positions, like up, down, front, and back.

Aniyah watched and whispered the moves to help her remember them. "Stomp, clap, stomp, clap, stomp-stomp, clap-clap. Right knee up, clap. Left knee up, clap. Right knee up, clap. Left knee up, clap. Clap front and stomp. Clap back and stomp. Dab up right, stomp left. Dab down right, stomp left. Dab up left, stomp right. Dab down left, stomp right. Stomp-stomp-stomp-stomp. Clap."

"Now do it again. This time, pick up the pace, and don't call the steps," said Ms. Soto.

The veterans nodded. Jasmine called, "Ready?"

The other girls in her line got in ready position.

"Ready, and . . ." Jasmine started.

A second later, the girls blasted through the routine, perfectly in sync. Their moves sounded like drums going *boom*, *boom*, and *rat-a-tat-tat*.

What had taken the new girls an hour to learn during the first meeting lasted a minute when put together—maybe less. When the leaders stopped, everyone cheered.

Ms. Soto raised her hands for attention. "This is only the beginning. Our full routine will be about seven minutes. We've got a lot of work to do before our competition. Everyone stand up and get in the ready position."

The rest of the girls scrambled to their feet. They all raised their arms and put their fists together.

"Jasmine will stay in front," Ms. Soto said. "The rest of my veterans, please join one of the other lines so you can help our new members."

For the rest of the practice, Jasmine slowly called out the steps, and everyone else followed. Again and again and again. During the final fifteen minutes, the girls tried to pick up the pace and run through the steps in real speed.

The first time through sounded like a school band during its warm-ups—chaos. The claps and taps and stomps happened randomly instead of in sync. At the end of the routine, they all laughed at themselves. Aniyah realized it was going to be hard to move at the same time, even when everyone had the basic moves memorized.

Soon, though, the group looked and sounded better. Many were getting the hang of it. But others, including Aniyah, still stepped or clapped at the wrong time.

Stacy, who was in the row in front of Aniyah, had it all memorized. At the end of one drill, Stacy bounced on her toes and clapped. "I did it!" Aniyah heard Stacy cheer to herself.

Stacy looked back at Aniyah, who smiled and gave her friend an air five. Aniyah loved that Stacy was so enthusiastic about everything. Her smile quickly faded, though, when Jasmine told them to get ready to do it again.

Ms. Soto slowly walked alongside each row and watched the girls perform. Aniyah's heartbeat sped up as Ms. Soto got closer.

Oh, no, she thought. *Ms. Soto is going to see that I'm not getting this. If I can't even perform in front of her, how am I ever going to be able to perform in front of a crowd and judges? How am I ever going to be as good as my mom?*

Aniyah's hands started to sweat, which made her clapping sloppy. She wiped her hands on the sides of her shorts and tried to catch up with the routine. But she was completely off track.

Aniyah stopped and bent over. She put her hands on her knees and closed her eyes tightly. She inhaled deeply and exhaled slowly.

A moment later, someone tapped her shoulder. Aniyah turned her head and opened one eye. Ms. Soto was looking at her with concern.

"Come over here," she said to Aniyah. She led Aniyah away from the other girls before she asked, "Is everything okay?"

"Not really," Aniyah admitted.

"Tell me what's going on," Ms. Soto replied.

"I'm nervous about competing and performing in

37

front of people," Aniyah said. Her words came out in spurts. "I joined with Stacy because I had promised her and because it was a club with no pressure. But, now we're a team, and all I can think about is performing in front of judges and crowds and my mom, who is a master stepper. I can't concentrate on the steps. I can only think about competing at some point, and that makes it hard to stay in sync with everyone else."

"Okay," said Ms. Soto. "Relax for a bit and breathe in and out, deeply and slowly."

Aniyah concentrated on her breathing until she felt calmer. Her heartbeat wasn't pounding in her ears anymore.

"Have you heard of the acronym W.I.N.?" asked Ms. Soto.

Aniyah shook her head.

"It stands for *What's Important Now*," said Ms. Soto. "The idea is to focus on the moment. Concentrate on what you have to do *now*. Don't worry about what comes next or what may happen tomorrow or next week or next year. If you do, you're wasting mental energy. You're worrying about something in the future that you can't control. Most of all, you're missing out on the present."

"I hear what you're saying, Ms. Soto," said Aniyah. "But that's easier said than done. I know I shouldn't worry, but I can't help it. I can't just turn off my nerves." She shook out her arms and wiped her palms on her shorts again.

"You're right," said Ms. Soto. "But there are things you can do to manage your nerves. Try the W.I.N. strategy and practice the steps at home. Do the routine in front of a mirror, all by yourself. Don't worry about being in sync with your teammates. Just get in sync with yourself." Ms. Soto smiled. "No one else will be in your room, so you won't be comparing yourself to others. Focus on the steps. Focus on the moment. Focus on you. That's all. Just you and the steps."

"Me and the steps. That's all," repeated Aniyah.

"That's right," said Ms. Soto.

"Okay, Coach. I'll try."

"'Coach.' I like the sound of that," Ms. Soto said with a smile. She turned to the other girls, and said, "From now on, call me Coach, since we are a team!"

The team exploded with whoops and cheers.

* * *

At home, Aniyah stood in front of the full-length mirror that hung on the back of her bedroom door.

"What's important now?" she said to herself. "What's important is that I master these steps, first slowly and then quickly. Focus on the steps and nothing else."

Aniyah took a few deep breaths and shook out her arms. She started the routine. She did each move slowly and named it out loud, just like Jasmine had during practice. She remembered each step.

"All right," she said and nodded. "Now a little faster." She did the routine again. At the end, she smiled at herself in the mirror. "Not bad at all."

She stopped to send a text message to Stacy:

I can't believe I'm saying this, but I think I'm getting the hang of the steps! It's actually fun now that I sort of know what I'm doing.

Stacy responded with a GIF of an entire stadium erupting in applause.

Aniyah smiled and went back to the mirror. "Let's try it again, faster this time," she said.

But this time, in the middle of the routine, the door opened. It nearly hit Aniyah in the face.

"Ugh. Mom!" Aniyah exclaimed.

"What? Am I not allowed to come into your room?" her mom asked.

"Of course you can come in—if you knock!" said Aniyah. "I was practicing, and I need the door closed so I can see myself in the mirror."

"Oh, sorry!" her mom said.

Aniyah thought her mom would leave. Instead, she came in and closed the door behind her.

"There," Mom said. "Now you can look in the mirror."

"But . . . you're still here," said Aniyah.

"Is that a problem?" asked her mom.

"Coach said I should practice by myself," said Aniyah.

"Yeah, but if you end up competing, then you're going to have an audience," Mom pointed out. "You might as well start with me!"

"Mom, you're not my coach," said Aniyah. She was trying to control her tone and temper, but she was getting more and more annoyed. "My *actual* coach said to practice alone. She wants me to focus on myself and the steps. She doesn't want me to worry about anyone or anything else."

"But I know stepping. I can give you advice!" her mom said cheerfully.

"I don't want your advice!" Aniyah snapped.

Regret immediately washed over Aniyah. On the one hand, she meant what she'd said. She wanted to follow her coach's advice and practice alone. She didn't want her mom's suggestions right now.

On the other hand, she knew that what she'd said and how she'd said it had hurt her mother's feelings.

Both Aniyah and her mom were quiet for a few uncomfortable moments.

"Got it," Mom finally said. She opened Aniyah's bedroom door and left the room, closing it softly behind her.

Aniyah plopped herself onto her bed and turned on the television in her room. She didn't feel like practicing anymore.

CHAPTER 5

RUNNING AND PUMPING IRON

At the next drill team practice, the girls ran through the first one-minute routine they'd learned. After three tries, everyone had it down perfectly. They celebrated the moment with cheers and high fives, which filled Aniyah with joy, pride, and belonging.

I did it! she thought. *I nailed the steps, and I didn't feel nervous!*

"That was great!" Coach Soto said. "This is the result of lots of practice, hard work, and focus."

Coach purposely locked eyes with Aniyah and nodded. Aniyah smiled. It felt good to be recognized. She had been practicing at home all weekend, and she'd been doing her best to focus, stay calm, and think W.I.N.

"Today, we'll start adding moves to build up to a full, seven-minute routine," said Coach Soto. "We have five weeks before our first competition."

The reminder that she only had one-seventh of the routine memorized deflated Aniyah a bit. And then the word *competition* made her stomach clench.

About halfway through practice, Aniyah pictured the judges, the crowd, and her mom watching her every movement. The joy she felt earlier was replaced with dread. When her chest felt tight, she stopped stepping and bent over. With her hands on her knees, she tried to catch her breath.

Coach Soto saw this. "Let's take a five-minute break," she called. She walked quickly over to Aniyah. "Are you okay?"

"I'm trying, Coach. I really am," said Aniyah. "I've been doing the W.I.N. thing and trying to focus on just me and the steps. But if I stay on the team, that means competitions. Then it's *not* just about me and the steps. I don't want to let the team down."

"Aniyah, you won't let anyone down, yourself included, as long as you do your best," said Coach Soto. "We'll add to the routine slowly, and we'll practice each part until everyone gets it. This is a team effort. You're not in this alone."

At that point, Stacy came over. She crouched down like a frog so she could see Aniyah's face.

"Hey!" she said, looking worried. "You okay?"

Aniyah stood up and linked her fingers behind her head, stretching her torso to help her breathe. Once she felt better, she wiped her eyes with the palms of her hands. She stood tall and put her fists on her hips, but her breathing was still a little ragged.

"I'm sorry, Aniyah," said Stacy, seeing her friend's struggle. "I pushed you into this. You don't have to stick with it if you really don't want to."

"The thing is, I think I want to stick with it," said Aniyah. "Nailing the steps at the beginning of practice felt so good. It was fun and cool, and I felt like I was a part of something."

Stacy and Coach Soto smiled.

"But I just don't know if I *can* do it," said Aniyah.

"Aniyah, do you have trouble breathing only when you're feeling anxious?" asked Coach Soto.

"Yeah, mostly," said Aniyah. "Although, after the first practice, I was panting because I was exhausted."

Coach nodded and then said, "Okay, so we have to tackle this on two fronts. For your nerves, continue to use the W.I.N. strategy."

"Okay. . . ," said Aniyah.

"And for your stamina, we're going to add cardio and strength training," said Coach.

"Wait . . . what?" asked Aniyah.

Instead of responding to Aniyah, Coach raised her voice and shouted, "Follow me, girls."

The girls exited the gym and followed Coach onto the track. Once there, Aniyah asked, "So, what are we going to do on the track?"

"Run," Coach replied.

"Run?" asked Aniyah.

"That's what people normally do on the track," said Coach Soto.

Aniyah was still confused. "Yeah, but why are we running? Shouldn't we be practicing new steps?"

"Part of being a good stepper is knowing how to control your breathing," said Coach. "When the club first formed, we came out here all the time. The girls couldn't step, clap, and chant if they were huffing and puffing like the big bad wolf."

Jasmine and the other veterans laughed.

Aniyah noticed she *was* breathing hard, just from jogging in spurts to keep up with Coach as she led them outside.

"Ready?" asked Coach.

The others shouted, "Ready!" while Aniyah mumbled, "Not really."

"Well," said Coach, "ready or not, here we go."

Coach took off, and Aniyah and the other steppers started after her. Aniyah noticed that some girls could jog around the quarter-mile track without stopping. Aniyah couldn't maintain a jog the whole time. When she felt her chest tighten, she slowed down to a walk.

When the girls were done running, Coach led them through some stretches. Jasmine, who was next to Aniyah, asked, "How are you feeling?"

"I'm beat," said Aniyah. She was breathing hard.

Jasmine nodded. "It'll get easier the more you do it, just like everything else," she said.

* * *

At the next practice, a note on the gym door told the girls to meet in the weight room. Once everyone arrived, Coach said, "We're here because you all need to build up your muscles. Stepping and jogging will get easier with some strength training. From now on, we'll either run or lift weights for part of each practice."

"Great," said Aniyah sarcastically as she started weighted leg lifts.

What she *didn't* say was that she wished she could rewind time back to her family's Labor Day party and take back her promise to Stacy. Stepping was one thing, but now she had running and strength training on top of it?

What did I get myself into? Aniyah worried.

CHAPTER 6

THE FIRST COMPETITION

Five weeks later, Aniyah did feel stronger. She didn't get out of breath as easily while stepping. Coach had been right. The addition of cardio and strength training had made stepping easier.

Aniyah realized that part of the reason why she had struggled to breathe during the earlier practices was probably a lack of physical conditioning.

During the past five weeks, she had also worked hard to become stronger mentally. Aniyah was training herself to focus on the moment and not worry about the future. After all, if she was actually going to go through with the first competition, she had to be strong in every way possible.

At the end of their last practice, when Aniyah had told Stacy that she'd decided to compete, her friend had nearly broken her eardrum with her scream of excitement.

Now, on the car ride to the first competition, Aniyah and Stacy ran through the routine in the back seat as best they could. They lightly stomped their feet on the floor and clapped or smacked the fronts or sides of their legs.

The girls had the steps for the full, seven-minute routine down cold. Aniyah had to admit that her confidence had grown week after week as the team had gotten better with each practice session. But the thought of performing for a crowd still made her nervous.

Aniyah's mom glanced at the girls in the rearview mirror. She didn't say anything or interrupt them. Her mom had barely said a word about stepping ever since Aniyah had snapped at her that day in her bedroom.

"We're almost there," announced Mr. Lewis from the passenger seat. "Are you girls excited?"

"Oh, yeah!" said Stacy.

"What about you, Niyah?" her dad asked.

"I know the steps, but I'm nervous," she admitted. "We didn't have an audience or judges during practice."

Aniyah's mom pursed her lips, but didn't say a word. Aniyah knew she was probably thinking, *Well, you could have practiced in front of a small audience at home. . . .*

When they arrived at the school hosting the competition, Aniyah and Stacy made their way to the cafeteria. Each team was assigned a table or two where they could leave their things and wait for their turn to compete.

Aniyah and Stacy joined their teammates at their assigned tables, but they were too antsy to stay seated. Everyone was full of nervous excitement as the competition began. One by one, groups were called into the gym to perform.

When Northwest Middle School was called, Coach Soto raised her hand and said, "Line up."

The girls followed Coach from the cafeteria to the gym's entrance. As the girls entered the gym, Coach Soto said something positive to each of them.

"You've got this," she said to Aniyah. "Remember W.I.N. and breathe!"

Aniyah nodded and exhaled the breath she was holding. She focused on the girl in front of her and no one else. She avoided looking at all of the people in the bleachers. Her parents were up there somewhere.

Ignoring all the noise was tough, though. The sounds of the cheering crowd made Aniyah's stomach somersault.

As she took her place in line, she inhaled deeply, shook out her arms, and wiped her hands on the sides of her black jeans. She looked down to make sure the laces on her black boots were tied. She also checked to see that her purple shirt was tucked in.

When Aniyah looked up, she caught a glimpse of the judges' table and felt a little dizzy. Again, she focused her eyes on the back of the girl in front of her.

What's important now is following the steps, Aniyah thought. *Listen for Jasmine's voice only. No one else's. Run through the routine like you've done a thousand times before.*

Aniyah heard Jasmine's voice rise above the crowd. "Ready!" she shouted.

The girls stood up straight. They raised their arms out in front of them and held their balled fists tightly together, in the ready position.

Aniyah could feel her pulse quicken as she waited for the cue that would start their seven-minute routine.

"Ready, and . . . ," Jasmine called.

"We are the Northwest Drill Team, and we break it down like this!"

Aniyah began the routine in sync with the others, but she soon lost focus. Instead of concentrating on the steps, she noticed the people in the crowd who were cheering for other teams. She caught a glimpse of her mom but couldn't read the look on her face.

Is she disappointed in me? she wondered. *Am I not a good enough stepper to carry on the family tradition?*

Aniyah's hands started to sweat, which produced sloppy claps.

The next part of the routine had a call-and-response chant.

Jasmine called: "We are Northwest!"

And the rest of the girls repeated it: "We are Northwest!"

"Don't mean to brag, but we are the best."

"Don't mean to brag, but we are the best."

"We didn't come to play."

"We didn't come to play."

"We came to step, so get out of our way."

"We came to step, so get out of our way."

Next, Aniyah stepped left instead of right because she was focused on a stern-looking judge who kept jotting notes on her score sheet. Aniyah's breathing came in short bursts, despite all of the cardio she had done. She knew her chest was tight because of her anxiety, not her physical conditioning.

When the entire routine was over, the girls jumped and cheered. But Aniyah didn't feel like celebrating. Those seven minutes had been brutal.

Coach Soto didn't seem to care about any of her mistakes. She hugged and high-fived all the girls.

"That was awesome!" Coach cheered. "I am so proud of all of you!"

Stacy, the other girls, and Aniyah's parents were all equally enthusiastic and complimentary about the team's performance, even though it only earned them a participation ribbon.

"I know you don't want my advice," Aniyah's mom said on the ride home. "But I have to say, you girls exploded with energy out there. You were amazing!"

"Yeah, great job, girls, especially for your first competition," said Mr. Lewis. "You're only going to get better from here."

Despite all of the positive comments, Aniyah felt emotionally defeated, as well as physically exhausted. She had spent six weeks stepping and running and lifting weights, practicing in front of the mirror in her room to memorize every step, and mentally training herself to stay focused and tune out negativity. And still . . . her anxiety had taken over and ruined everything.

Even after using the W.I.N. method, she felt like a loser. Aniyah quietly decided on the ride home that she was definitely going to quit the team.

CHAPTER 7

DON'T QUIT YET

The following Monday, the day of the next team practice, Aniyah went to Coach Soto's classroom during lunchtime.

"Come on in, Aniyah," Coach Soto said when she saw her in the doorway.

"I can't stay long," said Aniyah. "I just came by to tell you that I'm quitting the team."

Coach gave Aniyah a surprised look. She said, "Please have a seat, Aniyah."

Aniyah slid into a nearby desk chair.

"Tell me what's going on," said Coach. She came over from the whiteboard and perched on the edge of her desk.

"I'll admit that I didn't want to join in the beginning," said Aniyah. "I had promised Stacy I would go with her to the first meeting, and then my mom said I should at least go to the practices before the first competition. I honestly felt like it was something I *had* to do." Aniyah stopped to take a breath before going on.

"And now, the thing is, I *want* to do it. I really do. But I *can't*. My performance anxiety was so bad, I felt like I was going to pass out or throw up or both. Having my mom in the audience made it worse since she's such a good stepper. I'm worried about disappointing her."

"I can honestly say that you didn't *look* like you were going to pass out or throw up during the performance," Coach Soto said. "You looked great."

"Really?" said Aniyah. "My heart was pounding. My hands were sweating. I felt like every step and clap was a beat off."

"Your nerves made you think your performance was worse than it was," said Coach. "Did girls make mistakes? Yes. Did I expect that? Absolutely. Was I disappointed in our team? Absolutely not."

Aniyah smiled and thought about how Coach had hugged and high-fived every one of them after the competition, as if they had just won an Olympic gold medal. Aniyah knew that Coach was sincerely proud of them for completing their first competition, mistakes and all.

"I know the routines. I'm doing the workouts. I've practiced the W.I.N. strategy to help me focus, and I do the deep-breathing exercises," said Aniyah. "I don't know what else to try."

"Your anxiety may never go away completely," said Coach, "but with time and practice, you'll get more and more used to performing in front of a crowd. The first time was bound to be the scariest. And you should be so proud of yourself."

Aniyah shrugged and stared down at her shoes. She was not convinced that she could compete in front of an audience ever again.

"I would hate for you to walk away from something you want to do," said Coach. She tapped her chin thoughtfully. "Let me think about this, okay? If you stay on the team for now, I promise to come up with a plan to help you get more comfortable with performing."

Aniyah took in and let out a deep breath. She nodded and said, "Okay. Deal."

"Great," said Coach, and she gave Aniyah a big smile.

Aniyah stood up and slowly walked to the door. Before she left, she turned around and said, "Thanks, Coach."

CHAPTER 8

BUILDING SELF-CONFIDENCE

At practice a week later, Coach Soto got the girls' attention and then said, "Follow me." When she started walking toward the door, Aniyah figured they were heading to the track for more cardio training.

When they were all outside, though, Coach led them right past the track.

"Where are we going?" asked Jasmine.

"Wheeler Elementary School," said Coach.

The girls all exchanged looks.

"Why?" asked Jasmine.

"You'll see," Coach said. She continued walking.

When the team reached the elementary school two blocks away, Coach stopped at the front door. She turned around and said, "We're here because we need more practice performing in front of people. Everything feels different in front of strangers who are staring at you."

Aniyah smiled at Stacy and then looked at the other girls. She wondered if anyone else felt as nervous as she had during the first competition.

Maybe I wasn't the only one who needed to get control of my nerves, Aniyah thought.

"Here's the plan," said Coach. "You'll break up into teams of three and perform for different groups of elementary students in the after-school program. You'll start out with one group of students. Then you and those students will join up with another class and their performers. A team of three steppers will become six, then nine, and so on. The team of steppers and the audience will grow bigger each time. At the end, we'll meet in the auditorium and perform as a whole team for all the students."

Coach let all of the information sink in for a moment. "Make sense?" she asked.

"Yes, ma'am!" the girls answered.

It made sense to Aniyah. She needed more experience performing in front of people to build her confidence. She hoped this would work because she realized more and more how much she wanted to stay on the team.

Coach pulled a piece of paper out of her pocket and read the names of the girls in each group.

"Jasmine, Aniyah, and Stacy, you're starting in room three," said Coach.

Stacy did a little happy dance, showing her usual excitement.

"You should have joined cheerleading instead," Aniyah said to her.

"Maybe I'll do both," Stacy said with a wide smile. "Want to join me?"

"Absolutely not," said Aniyah with a laugh.

Aniyah and Stacy followed Jasmine through the door and down a long hallway. When the girls reached room three, they saw six first graders drawing at small round tables. The after-school monitor asked the students to leave their art projects and gather on the rug for the performance.

Aniyah and Stacy stood on either side of Jasmine. Jasmine naturally took the lead, like she always did during team practices.

I wonder if she was always this confident, thought Aniyah. *Was she nervous to walk into the gym for her first step practice? Will I ever be that confident?*

"Hi, everyone!" said Jasmine.

The group of first graders waved enthusiastically and shouted, "Hi!" back.

Aniyah couldn't help but laugh. They were all so squirmy, curious, and excited to have visitors. Aniyah realized with relief that it probably wouldn't be very hard to impress them.

Jasmine explained what stepping was in the most basic way. Then the three got in ready position.

"Ready, and . . ."

"We are the Northwest Drill Team, and we break it down like this!"

The first graders moved back and forth with the beat. Some clapped. One girl couldn't help but jump up and try to imitate the steppers. When the routine ended, the students all cheered.

"I wish the competitions were as easy as that was," whispered Aniyah.

"Well, during our next competition, imagine their happy little faces in the crowd," suggested Jasmine.

The girls headed to the next classroom to meet up with three other teammates. Their group of students trailed behind then.

In the next room, Jasmine stepped back and said, "Go ahead, Stacy, lead us off."

"No way, really?" whispered Stacy.

"Yeah, go for it."

Stacy moved forward. "Hi, I'm Stacy." She then turned and said, "Please introduce yourselves, ladies."

Jasmine cleared her throat and said, "Hi, I'm Jasmine," and then everyone looked at Aniyah.

An image of the crowd and the judges at the competition flashed in Aniyah's mind. She shook it away and focused on the cute, curious faces in front of her. She swallowed, cleared her throat, and said, "Hi, I'm Aniyah."

That wasn't so bad, she immediately thought.

Like Jasmine, Stacy then explained stepping and led them through the routine. And like before, the audience was on their feet cheering by the end of the performance.

Was the audience at the competition this enthusiastic?
Aniyah wondered. *I'm sure my parents were cheering for us, just like these kids are. Why didn't I notice that?*

The steppers and students moved from room to room, performing their routine two more times. Finally, they gathered in the auditorium.

Aniyah felt a little nervous standing on the stage with the lights shining on them. She wasn't panicked though. Her heartbeat was normal. Her hands weren't sweating. Coach's experiment had worked. Performing multiple times for different audiences had built her confidence.

I just hope I can feel this way during our next competition, Aniyah thought.

CHAPTER 9

ANIYAH'S TOUGHEST AUDIENCE

The night before the next competition, a month after their first, Aniyah was practicing in front of the full-length mirror behind her bedroom door. As she worked through the routine, she imagined her teammates around her, moving at the same time.

She also imagined a happy, cheering audience. In her mind, the judges weren't hard-faced. They were there to do a job, but they were as eager to see the routine as the elementary kids had been. Aniyah felt relaxed and confident when she visualized her teammates and a supportive environment.

When her mom knocked on the door, Aniyah stopped. "Come in," she called.

Her mom entered the room carrying a folded stack of clean clothes. "Sorry to interrupt," she said. "I have laundry for you."

"Thanks," said Aniyah.

"Does Stacy need a ride to the competition tomorrow?" her mom asked.

Aniyah shook her head. "No, her mom doesn't have to work this weekend, so she can drive her."

Mom placed the clean clothes on Aniyah's bed and turned back toward the door.

"Mom, wait," said Aniyah. "I'm sorry for snapping at you when I first joined the team. I know you were only trying to help. But I wasn't ready to have you watching me and judging me."

"Oh, Aniyah," her mom replied. "I wanted to help you, not judge you."

"I know that now," said Aniyah. "Back then, though, I wasn't ready to do my routine in front of you because of my anxiety and because I didn't want to disappoint you. At the first competition, I was a mess."

"You didn't look like a mess," said her mom. "You looked pretty good, actually."

"Thanks," said Aniyah. "Yeah, Coach and everyone else said we did okay. I *felt* like a hot mess, though. In my head, I wasn't doing anything right. My nerves took over, and I couldn't see anything in a positive light."

"I understand," said her mom. "I really do. What about now? Are you feeling more confident?"

Aniyah took a deep breath. "Yeah, I am. It gets easier the more we practice."

"Makes sense," her mom said.

"Actually, if you and Dad are willing to watch me, that would be really helpful. I'd love any last-minute advice you have before tomorrow's competition."

Her mom smiled widely. "Really?"

"Really," said Aniyah. "Get Dad, and I'll meet you in the living room."

A few minutes later, Aniyah's parents sat on the living room couch. Aniyah stood in front of them in the ready position. For the first time, she called out, "Ready, and . . ."

Aniyah imagined her teammates around her as she ran through the full routine. She did both the call and response parts of the chants and stomped and clapped at full speed.

Her stomach clenched in a tiny knot, but she wasn't breathing hard or sweating. She knew her nerves would never go away completely, but her focus wasn't on her audience. She wasn't thinking that every move was all wrong. She was focused on the steps and claps and rhythm—nothing else.

When Aniyah finished, her parents whistled and cheered for her. As Aniyah caught her breath, her mom asked, "So, how do you feel?"

"I feel good," Aniyah said with a smile. Her pulse pounded from pride, not nerves. "Do you have any advice?"

Mom shook her head. "Honestly, no. You look strong and confident. You hit your moves with attitude and precision. And you looked like you were having fun. I'm really proud of you."

"Looks like you and your sisters will have some competition at the next Labor Day party," said Aniyah's dad. "A new generation of steppers is ready to take you on."

"Bring it," her mom said with a smile. "We'll be ready."

"We don't need to compete, Mom. You and my aunties can teach Stacy and me some of *your* moves."

"Deal," said her mom.

CHAPTER 10

WE CAME TO STEP

Aniyah mentally ran through the routine one more time as her parents drove to the competition.

"How are you feeling?" her mom asked. She glanced at Aniyah in the rearview mirror as she drove.

"I'm okay," said Aniyah.

She had a normal level of nerves, but she definitely felt much better than the first time the team had competed. Now she knew what to expect. The moves had become second nature, and she had more experience performing in front of people.

The team gathered in the cafeteria and waited for their turn. Coach Soto told them to huddle up.

"Remember the word *Umoja*," said Coach Soto. "When you step, you are unified. You are athletes. You are musicians, making music with your bodies. You are teammates. You are sisters."

Coach stretched out her arm into the middle of the huddle. Each of the girls stretched out an arm and placed one hand on top of another.

"No matter what happens today, I am proud of you," said Coach. "Umoja on three. One, two, three!"

"UMOJA!" they all yelled.

The girls lined up to walk into the gym. This time, Aniyah looked around without feeling overwhelmed. She spotted her parents sitting next to Stacy's mom. They clapped and hooted as the girls got into lines and the ready position.

Jasmine called out, "Ready, and . . ."

A second later, in one, loud voice, the team chanted, "We are the Northwest Drill Team, and we break it down like this!"

They blasted through the first part of the routine, the very first moves Aniyah had learned. There were stomps and claps, knees-up claps, followed by dabs up and down the other side. It was all accompanied by *stomp-stomp-stomp*. The girls' moves were precise and in sync, their bodies sounding like percussion instruments.

Aniyah did a quick self-check. Her breathing was fine. No sweaty palms. She smiled and was ready for the next set of moves. She tuned out the noise of the crowd and put everything she'd learned into the routine.

"We are Northwest!" Jasmine called.

"We are Northwest!" the team responded.

Since the last competition, the girls had added moves between each call and response. They dropped into a low squat, hit the top of their thighs, and clapped between each one.

"Don't mean to brag, but we are the best."

"Don't mean to brag, but we are the best."

They popped back up. Still stomping, they repositioned into a single-file line. As they chanted, they alternated stomps and windmill moves to the left and right.

"We didn't come to play."

"We didn't come to play."

"We came to step, so get out of our way. . . ."

Here, they alternated, one girl sliding to the right, another to the left, until they were in two lines. They dropped down and hit the floor in front of them, then popped up, knees high, stomping hard as each foot came back to the ground.

Aniyah accidentally stomped right when everyone else stomped left, but it didn't stop her. She quickly recovered and finished on the right step.

For the rest of the routine, Aniyah stayed focused and in control of her moves and breathing. She worried a little that her mistake would hurt the team's score. The thought didn't haunt her, though. She stomped it away with her next step.

This time, when their performance ended, Aniyah celebrated along with her teammates. She had done the best she could, and she didn't feel dizzy or sick to her stomach.

That was a W.I.N. in her book!

After all the teams had performed, the P.A. system started to crackle. The announcer called all the teams back into the gym for the results.

The Northwest Drill Team huddled together near the bleachers and held hands.

"In third place, let's give a round of applause to Lakeside Middle School!" the announcer said.

The girls stopped holding hands so that they could clap for the other team.

The announcer started up again and said, "In second place . . . " The girls gripped hands again. "Let's give a round of applause to Northwest Middle School!"

The girls exploded with excitement. They jumped and screamed and hugged one another. They had placed second! Most of the dozen other teams had been competing for years. Second place was a major accomplishment.

Aniyah jumped up and down some more and then hugged every one of her teammates and Coach Soto. The girls then nudged Coach forward so that she could accept the team's first trophy.

When she returned with it, Coach was pulled into a big group hug. The girls bounced up and down and chanted, "We are Northwest! We are Northwest!"

Aniyah bounced and chanted along with them. She was filled with pride that she was part of something. She remembered Coach's words before the competition.

I am an athlete. I am a musician. I am a teammate. These are my sisters. We are unified in movement and purpose. Umoja.

Aniyah finally understood her mom and aunties' passion for this sport. She understood the bond they felt when they stepped together. Stepping was their thing, and now it was Aniyah's thing too.

ABOUT the AUTHOR

 Cindy L. Rodriguez is the author of the young adult novel *When Reason Breaks* and *Volleyball Ace* from the Jake Maddox JV series. She also contributed to the anthology *Life Inside My Mind: 31 Authors Share Their Personal Struggles.* Before becoming a teacher, she was an award-winning reporter for *The Hartford Courant* and researcher for *The Boston Globe*'s Spotlight Team. She is a founder of Latinxs in Kid Lit, a blog that celebrates children's literature by/for/about Latinxs. Cindy is a big fan of the three Cs: coffee, chocolate, and coconut. She is currently a middle school reading specialist in Connecticut, where she lives with her family.

GLOSSARY

acronym (AK-roh-nim)—a word formed from the first letters of other words, such as W.I.N. (What's Important Now)

anxiety (ang-ZYE-uh-tee)—a feeling of worry or fear

cardio (KAHR-dee-oh)—having to do with the heart

generation (jen-er-AY-shun)—a group of people born around the same time

gumboot dance (GUHM-boot DANSS)—a South African dance performed by dancers wearing rubber boots, often with attached bells that ring as the dancers stomp

master (MASS-ter)—to become very skilled

percussion (per-CUSH-uhn)—instruments that create sound when they are struck or shaken

precision (prih-SIH-zhun)—exact accuracy

routine (roo-TEEN)—a series of moves done in a particular order in a performance

synchronized (SING-kruh-nizd)—when two or more people perform the same movements at the same time

unified (YOO-nih-fide)—brought together as one

DISCUSSION QUESTIONS

1. Aniyah feels pressure from her family to carry on the step tradition. Where does the story show us that step teams are a big part of Aniyah's heritage?

2. Coach Soto tries to help Aniyah overcome her performance anxiety. Do you agree with the strategies she used? Can you suggest other strategies Aniyah might have tried?

3. Aniyah and Stacy have a strong friendship. Think of some examples from the story that show each of them giving support to the other.

WRITING PROMPTS

1. Aniyah is excited and nervous about the energy in the gymnasium at the first competition. Imagine you are there. Write a paragraph describing the sights, sounds, and feelings of being in that gymnasium.

2. Aniyah is frustrated when her mom interrupts her practicing in her bedroom. Do you think Aniyah could have handled the situation differently? Rewrite the conversation between Aniyah and her mother to have a different outcome.

3. Step teams use a lot of call-and-response chants to get the crowd engaged. Come up with your own call-and-response chant. Include your school name or the name of your favorite dance or sports team. See if you can come up with a rhyme for each line.

MORE ABOUT THE SPORT

Stepping originated in Africa and was heavily influenced by the African gumboot dance. Gumboot dancers wear Wellington boots, commonly called gumboots, which may be decorated with bells that ring as the dancers stomp. The sounds made by stomping created a code used for communication. Black miners were not allowed to talk while working, so they used this stomping code to communicate with one another. Gumboot dancing is still performed by African performers.

Stepping was established in the United States in the 1900s at historically Black colleges and universities. Greek fraternities and sororities formed teams and performed at Step Shows to show pride in their Greek organizations and cultural roots.

Stepping has elements of dance, military marching, and call and response. It is considered both a sport and an art form. It is a dancelike performance that requires stamina and power and blends African folk traditions with popular culture.

When stepping, the body becomes an instrument. Steppers make sounds by clapping, stomping, and speaking. Some drill teams also include elements of tap dancing, break dancing, and gymnastics.

Step and drill teams have been featured in movies and television shows. The Opening Ceremony of the 1996 Summer Olympics in Atlanta, Georgia, featured stepping. Beyoncé included stepping at her 2018 Coachella performance. Also in 2018, Lizzo performed a song called "Healing," alongside the award-winning Northside Step Team, as part of a Girls Who Code project for International Day of the Girl.

FOR MORE AWESOME
DANCE ACTION
PICK UP . . .

capstonepub.com